Whose footprint is that?

with Beatrice the beaver

created and illustrated by
Jacqui Brown

Beatrice the beaver
was building
a dam across the river.
She had collected
lots of branches, but
she needed one more.

So she went
to cut down
one more branch.

When Beatrice came back,
she saw that
a branch had disappeared.
She saw a large footprint, too.

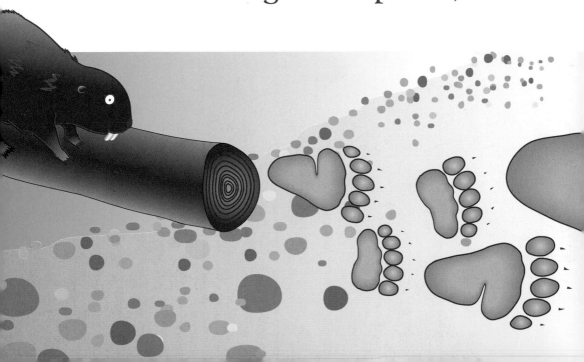

"Whose footprint is that?" wondered Beatrice.

There was a trail of footprints. Who had left the footprints? Beatrice decided to find out.

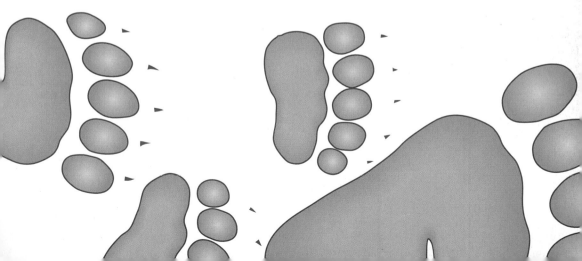

The first footprints
that Beatrice found
were not the right ones.
They had no toes.

But who had left them?

Gregory the goose
had left the footprints.

He liked to travel
long distances.

The next footprints
that Beatrice found
were too round.

But who had left them?

Wilma the wolf had left them.

She often howled all night.

The next footprints
that Beatrice found
were too small.

But who had left them?

Silvester the skunk
had left them.

He could be a bit smelly!

The next footprints
were not right at all.
The back prints were too long.
The front ones were too short.

But who had left them?

Ruby the rabbit
had left these footprints.

She liked
to hop, skip, and jump.

The next footprints
that Beatrice found
were definitely not
the right ones.
They were split
down the middle.

But who had left them?

Maurice the moose
had left them.

He liked
to show off
his antlers.

At last Beatrice found
some large footprints.
And there was her branch.

"These are the right footprints,"
said Beatrice.

But who
do you think
had left them?

Ben the bear
had left the footprints.

"Why did you take my
branch?" Beatrice asked Ben.

"I'm sorry," said Ben.
"I wanted it as a fishing pole."

"I need the branch
for my dam," said Beatrice.
"But I will make
a better fishing pole for you."

"Oh, thank you," said Ben.
"I will help you
with your dam."

Ben often helps Beatrice
with her dam now.
Beatrice makes
all Ben's fishing poles, but
she never eats
his fish!